BURNING

poems for resistance

Avery Cassell

Pony Paws Press - 2025

Burning: poems for resistance

Pony Paws Press
Greenfield, MA 01301 USA
stoicpress.bigcartel.com
averystoicpress@gmail.com

Burning: poems for resistance/Avery Cassell
ISBN: 979-8-9887469-4-2

Cover designed by Avery Cassell
Back cover is a map of the Underground Railroad

Pony Paws Press

Dedication

Burning: poems for resistance is dedicated to San Francisco and to the Western Massachusetts Wednesday Night Writers Workshop.

TABLE OF CONTENTS

We Don't Admit What We Miss

I'm crouched in the sand
an ocean of dreams before me
waves tumbling in, washing my feet
tears and broken shells nest between my toes
speckled nightmares.

Nighttime and the moon shimmers
ghosts and squirrels cavort
thumping, rustling in the darkened rooms
I wander in my flannel robe
switching lights on and off.

I dreamt that I owned a tin can phone
butcher's twine laced between the two cans
diced tomatoes and pinto beans
I drilled a hole between our bedrooms
mouse tail size in diameter
at 5am I called you
for an early morning waffle date
you didn't pick up.

What I mean to say is,
you never picked up.
did mobsters crush your fingers
was your mouth too full of rat's nests and spite
did they forget to give you eyes
when you were in the womb?

Nighttime and the moon shimmers
a pearl hung by wishes
I speak to the ghosts
"I have stories" I tell them
I hold an empty can of beans to my ear
They whisper back, "We know."

LA *is Burning*

I can hear LA burning
all the way from Massachusetts
the screams whipping through my porch slumping
over drifts of snow
the crackle of a thousand fires
a thousand feet
hitting the ground running
oh, California! my broken heart.

Who's fiddling while the city burns?
red spittle from his lips, bubbles
a bloody tantrum
ketchup flying, splatter.

Strings breaking as the violin sighs
the whistle of flames turning the corner California
flexing, twisting
curling at the edges
a red fortune fish in my damp palm, our future
unsteady.

We're an orb of dirt and water
stumbling tumbling
fires and floods
blizzards and droughts
bellowing flames
scorching our future
with fuel from our past.

Orlando, June 12, 2016
To Mark Eitzel and our sacred hearts

I am trite. Nothing.
Today is divided
 into those who say "Orlando" and
see the past
and those who say "Orlando" and see the future.

Will the word "pulse" ever be the same?
a slithery kind of feeling
people in my office
talk about summer vacations
beach novels and bottles of wine
like nothing ever happened. Ever.
me, I'm nothing
listening. A walking target
my sacred heart.

It's like this, you see
at night you look up
look up!
you see shining stars in the sky
rising dancing higher, so far up
from Orlando on up like swirling
rising bloody clouds from the dance-floor
until stars cover the heavens
heaven has been covered with death
I avert my eyes because the sky is too bright
the blood falling, falling

4

back to earth, watering my anger
with their lives.

Who names the stars?
I need to talk to them today
tell them to get cracking
because we need to do some renaming.
Now.

You!
I live in a house made of your secrets
I walk barefoot on the rugs
woven of your shame
I choke on the dust that rises
rises, covering my skin
I breathe in your fear
I have promises
I am holding you hostage
holding sounds gentle
it's not love
it's not
you live in my anger.

No matter how much I ever tried
I've never passed for something not twisted
now we know that
neither did you
never passed at all.

I'm at work today
a lump of raw meat
in my office writing this
my office-mates oblivious
conversation ebbing in and out
their words dither into my room.

The gun control filibuster was last night
I watched, knitting
knitting for my life
a spool of rainbow wool unfurling into the night
a background of self-absorbed young queers
with their selfies and dim glooming
tweeting #queerselflove
damn you, wake up!
walk outside of yourself
the world needs you and you need it
but you sprinkle glitter on it and call it a day
turning from your elders.

And I'm still a gimp
a walking target
rags falling from my flesh, I stoop
losing my wallet, my keys, my thoughts
losing so much as I fall into the starry night.

Cake on Election Day

I'm going to willfully believe in cake
the soft bunny belly of kitties
hot ginger tea in a red mug
dogs rolling in freshly mowed grass
my two fingers slippery between my legs
curried coconut cauliflower simmering
steaming
filling the air with dinner
my birthday in three days
where I'll finally be old enough to know better
and yes, more cake.

I'm eating cake every day
for the next 31 days
the sugary crumbs coating my tongue
sweetening my words
so nothing bitter drips forth.

On November 8th
I'll open up
roaring what is trapped
the sound of 31 days of cake exploding.

Blackened

We are the darlings
inevitable, with blackened wings
we swoop through time
diving in and out of memories
they cling to us, gummy and bittersweet
we fly effortlessly
our bodies expansive
mammatus clouds
as dense as dreams
weaving through our limbs.

Fascism in the City

Threading memories from a park bench
to the sweet expanse of grass
damp, tickling my face
I inhale the Groundhog Day
spring of San Francisco
ice cream, always ice cream
pigeons and children
the twilight murmur of voices
speaking Spanish, Chinese, Thai
Mandarin, Persian, English.

Some wearing quilted vests
delicately clasping their phones
a benediction in their curled palms
I step around sleeping homeless men
snores in rising souring curls
crumpled coffee cups, nylon sleeping bags
mildewed in the salt and fog
my booted foot rising dreamily
the yellow smell of piss and money
jasmine and putrescence entitlement
housemates to the apocalypse
and yet, we drink tea and eat cake.

Scruffy, wearing overalls
cuffs rolled high and deep
wandering lopsided over the dunes
scrambling the pathways at Sutro Baths

never realizing that the end was coming
a lurid vintage paperback cover
spaceships, gams, and guns
disguising the future with muted colors
seedy, my empty knapsack flung carelessly
filled with salads and nuts
knitting projects and unread books
manuscripts if I'm productive.

Sickness arriving cheek by jowl with fascism
first, an incremental trickle
my tidy life dissolving
as we disintegrated
the journey marked by bleakness and beauty
there was always a slippery sexiness
magnolias and ferns as tall as my head
a nippy sardine laid across a crostini
is it any wonder that I became dizzy
a flâneur sprawled across my favorite green bench
the wood splintered, warmed by the sun
while I sought love and wonderment.

I walked and walked
over grey sidewalks and through dank bowers
glaring at cars, bikes, and scooters
I crossed the city streets
stomping, looking side-to-side
"don't you fucking look at me"
as city workers massacre the ficus trees
my heart fading, failing

the bloody mass shrugging its shoulders
until the dog finally caught its tail
releasing a deluge of masks and death.

Folding World, April 2021

The world is folding inside itself
an oyster
death, salty on my tongue
outside my bedroom window
a flowering cherry tree
a mile away, hospitals without room
for the corpses.

A morning April snow
clinging to the weeping cherry blossoms
flakes of icy tears
the sky a turgid smoke grey
I, with cat and coffee
beneath my quilt
watching.

Little Manhattan of the West, I

Little Manhattan of the West
built of tinted glass and artisanal kale
cleverly hand-crafted – you know the lingo
priced beyond the budget
of the ladies on the bus
shopping bags of eggs, cereal, and flowers
pinching dollars as they bleed
making a soup of hunger.

This week you arrogantly demand love
for your twee sensibilities
your liberal authentic sincerity
your flatly blatant shallowness is stunning
but I'm easily stunned
from poppers to patchouli to campfire cologne
you root through cellars
looking for great armfuls of culture
culture with elongated syllables
to cultivate in your kitchen, your head, your heart
tramping down Market Street
in your elegant velvet slippers
your torn sneakers
your polished leather boots
always changing, always changing.

now, the gleaming ice buses prowl the street
always clean and gliding silent doors

like elevator music and chaste socialites
something quiet
like dead fireflies after a midnight picnic
cloth shoes slipping down the steps
to scurry into your glass houses
sometimes swarming in Delores Park
drinking PBR and toothily sprawled
across the park, a hair coat woven
by sad-eyed women in Marin
I want to grab you by your twig bird-nest beard
a handful of your ratty hair
woven in a collage of Frieda Kahlo homage
I hiss "will you ever stop taking up so much fucking
space?"

I meditate these days
in bed with my heating pad tuned on high
take photos of alien waxy fatsia japonica
construction cranes lifting phallic metal pipes
into the cornflower blue morning
write and remember that I used to flirt
admire the lilting sensuous hills
of sandy dirt and salty sea smell
as the glass monoliths rise.

A lesson is this; everything is temporary
someday you'll look up
from the glass in your palm
your earbuds will tumble
out of your baby shell ears

your child's shit filled diaper
will slam you into 10am
faster than a fixie
rushing down Haight Street
the stink of the bus
chasing you into your building
someday this aching growth
won't matter anymore.

The tinted glass will be old hat
the kale will have wilted
you tilt your grey felt fedora forward
frisky oblivious into the night
stoned on atonality and preciousness
you don't need to believe me
I'm disparagingly blithe
and on bad days I don't believe me
we will be something different
Be. Something. Different.

The glass buildings, the hard streets
the trees waving in the fog
our feet running
running away from the ghosts of our past
we're the ghosts of our future
We're running through the streets
one replaces the other
the present is the past
the future is here and you are home.

Little Manhattan of the West, II

December and it starts to rain
like it hasn't been raining in forever
or at least since this drought started
it's winter in San Francisco
the rain pouring
water reflecting at night in the city streets
red and green lights flashing
on the black glistening pavement.

At first we laugh at the bus stop
unprepared for the whoosh of wet and cold, but
happy
we're children, holding our faces up
letting the water splash over our pink cheeks
I share my umbrella with a man
who's bringing hot pizza home to his wife
his hands dripping and the box steaming.

After a week people give up
I mean not me - I'm stoic
I return from work, my coat warm
scurry home
hunker down with soup, Swedish mysteries, and
my cat
safe in my Victorian hovel
I mean my damp apartment.

I'm riding the streetcar downtown
past Twitter and NEMA apartments
that black monolith studio Batcave
Twitter rising, it's Art Deco stateliness
Christmas season
the new tech offices have doormen
looming flat glass doors
it's Christmas in the lobbies
each Twitter Iowa farm boy channeling his
grandfather
erecting the biggest tree on the block, oh boy
erecting a tree in the center of
the vast shining grey marble lobby floor
a towering fir tree strewn with white lights
it's magical.

Looking through the streetcar window
a sheet of gleaming rain
the Christmas trees shine inside the offices like a
1940s movie
I expect to see wool suits and lush showgirls
Gene Kelly tap dancing with his reflection
twirling elfin around lamp posts
but all I see are pale bearded hipsters
in plaid and coffee
next to homeless men hunched
bleakly covered in plastic.

6pm on December 11th
I'm on the streetcar at night
to get Christmas balls from Cliff's in the Castro
when the transit inspectors board to check tickets
it's the worst night for rain thus far
novelty has worn off
everyone is cold and wet
social workers corralling homeless people
into churches to keep dry
tramps are riding the streetcar
to stay warm
the one across from me is wrapped in an army
blanket
miserable and defeated
the fare inspector in his navy uniform
uncomfortable in his power
writing him a ticket
ushering him off the streetcar into the dark rain
there's no singing in the rain
tap dancing around street lights here.

Avalon tore down the community garden
behind my apartment building
to erect a glass and faux wood apartment building
where the rent for the cheapest studio costs more
than my annual income
I'm not too bitter or bemused
well, maybe a little.

18

Erected a glossy apartment
tore down the plants in the garden
bringing cockroaches
scurrying from the dirt construction
glad to find a new home
where they were fed buttered toast and pie
but when a construction truck
plowed into our foundation
leaving an eight foot gash
the building shook
and with this rain streaming down
you can see where this is going
the outside pouring into our building
like we were a studio shopping cart home
steam rising
damp, mildew and mold into our 1906 building
which creaked and swelled and stank
while Avalon sat on their asses
leaving the gash gaping
a wound in our building.

The SROs are being converted into tech
communes
One Taste moves kitty-corner from Twitter
One Taste, the clit diddling cult with its
mysterious grammar;
Love, Your Orgasm
shopping cart homes piled with rags and plastic
leaking syringes and sorrow

hunched over pushing their home
past One Taste
past Twitter
past the bike shops, the coffee shops, the wine
bars
past the outdoor food court
with guards letting people in or not
girls and boys playing ukuleles and harmonicas
behind security fencing
swaying, sad almost folk music
artisan, sustainable, bacon, curry, grilled cheese
hand mother fucking crafted.

I don't understand living
walking to Nick's Grocery
for celery and eggs on a Sunday morning
past a regular next to his shopping cart home
bleary in the morning damp
wrapped in nylon quilted sleeping bags
one tramp already with his works out
shooting up into his leg
while his friend snores
I look
his white skin speckled with sores and freckles,
but hairless
he's intent
we don't meet one another's eyes
winter does this to me
no looking
no looking.

I don't understand living
how you can swig your artisanal coffee
while people are homeless?
how can I write this letter to my city?

Your sorrow pours like rain from the sky
a pigeon wing fluttering in the park
flapping their song noisily
Hayes Valley's barefoot homeless artist
scattering stale bread crumbs
washing his socks in a white plastic bucket
next to the playground
while women with big glasses and lank hair
eat made-to-order ice cream
small batch using liquid nitrogen
dainty kitten lapping
while reciting manifestos about fashion
I walk behind two 26 year old tech bros
discussing new sofas
one just got a $100,000 annual raise
which is more than I make
have ever made
I stumble over a crinkle in the sidewalk
thinking about that fact.

This city is now for you
you with the $3,500 studio penthouse, grubby
sneakers, homegrown attitude
what do you want?

do you want to change the world?
do you want to create art?
do you want to make more money than your
father?
your grandfather?
do you want to make love?
you've become part of a machine that is grinding
up our people
our sidewalks, our trees, our theater, our sex, our
children
maybe you say, "no, no, no"
shaking your head with your knit cap flapping in
the breeze
like puppy ears
you cross your arms belligerently
you're not part of that system no siree
if you were it isn't your fault and fuck them
anyway
because you're better, you're different, you're right.

The meaning of our city is money
little yipping dogs snipping at my heels
snarling, dripping greed
they erect new buildings gleaming black and green
glass facades mock everything you could imagine
mock wood, mock granite, mock marble
cheap coffee tables turned on their sides
Danish modern on an IKEA budget
the oblivious cost of life and death.

Little Manhattan of the West, III

The flowers that bloom in the spring tra-la!
It's a murky morning in San Francisco
past the curled up like locust sleeping homeless
this sidewalk is his home
sleeping, covered with a threadbare
scrap
not even a felted moving pad
or sleeping bag
a blanket.

Half a block down is the new apartment building
called Avalon
and as I write this at night
safe and snug, no bugs but
cat on lap
washing her fur
the clang of beggars collecting bottles
beneath my window
drunken Biergarten kitty-corner
yodeling over the night
over the locust homeless man
that sleeps one block away
curled into a question mark
who used to love him?
who loves him now?
not Avalon like the island
no swords here and nothing mystical

not even like Avalon the song
walking home romantic in the dark
I spy with my little eye
a candle in the rain
pile-upon-pile-upon-pile
will it ever stop?

The flowers this spring are plenty
sprouting *Now Hiring* signs
fades, tattered in windows
so hopeful
but stores, cafes, restaurants
are collapsing upon themselves
no one can afford to work here;
the commute
long hours and less money
stinking standing on the underground
as it brings you home
holding on, hanging on
hanging on.

What about the last one standing?
do any of you care?
how did your mother raise you?
records are kept on Facebook
we can curl up with coffee
and horror in the morning
you toss another empty champagne bottle
at workers cleaning Dolores Park
leaving the debris for whoever

like your mom
who's walking five steps
five steps behind you
while comforting you with tales
tales about Avalon where you're the king
the money green champagne bottle is a sword
you're the king
your army is fireflies in July
in a midwestern backyard
chasing girls. Oh my love.

The Lexington closed;
the last lesbian bar in the city.
Lucky 13 closed;
beloved dive.
Bibliohead Bookstore closed;
neighborhood used books.
Marlene's drag bar closed;
with his Santa collection guarding us.
Marcus's Bookstore closed;
the country's oldest black owned bookstore.
the downtown chess players banned
naked guys in the Castro banned
Mission Street venders ticketed
Folsom's date moved for a techie conference
soccer fields conquered by tech bros.

We disappear like sinkholes gulped 7/11
the largest monster size down your throat
you swallow neighborhoods piecemeal;

the Mission, Chinatown, Civic Center
we feel the lick of your tongue
as you devour us from
our homes to our cafes to our jobs.

Burning down the house
so many changes that I can't fucking keep track
any more
the fires are cleaning the underbrush
in the Mission
homes taken down by flames
and we are charred beneath your feet,
blackened, flopping in our dying throes
muscles and sinews stretched like rubber bands
melting.

Burning down the house
show tunes run through my head
springtime for Hitler
out with the old, in with the new
clear out the underbrush
you can't hide
oh fuck, did I say that?
buildings burn down to make room
for more tilted cheaply made apartments
more dueling champagne magnums
we throw bottles, gasoline
a cocktail for resistance
burning down the house.

Christmas Eve

Christmas Eve in San Francisco
it's 4:15pm, already getting dark
I'm on the prettiest streetcar driving
past whoever is left tonight at 6th and Market
self-righteous chocolatiers
elbowing out bums that have lived here
hell, all their life.

Between the pawn shop and the hipster food
court
I watch you yelling off the holidays
the unseasonable chill ripping at your mood
there isn't enough Mad Dog to keep neediness at
bay
the people that are left on Christmas eve
are the ones that can't get away
screaming in front of the shit pawn shop
a jumble of drum sets, drills, wedding bands in the
window
"motherfucker, fagget, ass-licker cunt"
everyone else fled
to families they'll complain about.

Wool sweaters and Virginia ham and money
so much money
skateboards and quilts and appetizers

the smooth glide of opening oven doors to check
on the pie.

While here you open the oven door to heat your
apartment
because it's cold
and the heater's for shit
with the paint peeling and mice nibbling
a slice of stale day-old sweet potato pie
with a glass of Early Times
and it's Christmas Eve.

A Wink of a Hat

Things change at the wink of a hat
I mean to say
here today – here tomorrow
and never close enough to hold
onto.

The wind, a whiff of spring
of white flowers delicately cloy
some kind of leaf spicy and pungent
a mantle of the future whenever I'm near.

The moon rising
a disc of light to bath under
a pearl so luminescent
that it sticks in my eyes
my heart shatters with beauty.

I want to say to you
harshness is not worth forbearance
our hearts full of tears and mystery
take that blanket of jasmine and moonlight
laid over us gently, so sweet
slumber together with me tonight.

Chatter of Crows

A scatter of words raining past
we're the crumbs beneath your feet
the poppy seed between your back molars
that your swollen tongue ineffectively probes.

I'm reduced to bleak sentences
that convey little besides a guttural "no"
"not enough" the crow whispers
beak chattering in my ear
where have you taken my country?

My body is inflamed
the Baker's cyst on my knee a knot
filled with anger and promises
I'm remembering the past
memories that forgot to be a dream.

The deep periwinkle night sky
lies to me
whispering that they're my lover
an elemental pillow
easing my heart
crows fly into my open window
their blackened wings silken
I roll over, open my covers
invite them in.

Nimble Bones

Your bones are delicate, pointed
nimble, they fly into the air
joyous, lighter than feathers
sharp as your tongue
bitter like a fairy tale from an icy country.

I huddle, pick them up
excitedly and tossing
throw your thin white bones skywards
they rest tipsy in the clouds
tilting through the ether
before tumbling scattered to my feet
your bones
a fortune teller's tiny trick.

Serendipitous Meeting on a Streetcar

The streetcar was filled with children
the rickety orange one from Milan
rush hour air filled with clanking, shouting, and
giggles
which I crankily tried to ignore.

Opposite was a fey gentleman
oval nails, a rhinestone cuff, and knickers
and two pigtailed seven-year-olds in pink
trying to peer out of one small dirty glass window
sharing a set of earbuds.

I was late for work, as always
when we got stuck at Market and 7th in the rain
in front of the Wednesday farmers market
the back door jamming and me sighing
my neighbor whooshing out a
flurried huff of impatience
kids screaming, queers fidgeting
and me knowing I'd be late again.

When like Rudolph on Xmas the savior
a butch arrived through the broken back door
a backpack of chard, leeks, and flowers
she sat beside me
christening me with irises
her silver hair sprinkled with raindrops

and me speechless with good fortune
feeling lucky, so lucky
her warm thigh pressed next to mine
jammed together, surrounded by cacophony
this handsome, middle-aged woman beside me
the streetcar starting again with a jolt,
as we smashed into one another's arms
flower petals caressing my cheek.

A Spell

The coup spreads its wings and struts
preening with anger and pride
the shiny feathers stiff, plastic
a child's costume headdress
in bloody red tipped with yellow bile
chomping words
adjectives and nouns dangling
from its beak like spittle.

A sour victory that I gather
I'm a witch and am watching you
your bitter hatred will throttle you
the pointed feathers will turn inward
you'll choke on outlawed words
your mangled body twitching.

Countdown

Things to be fearful of
one, two, three…

Bird flu and mystery pandemics
Kennedy and vaccine bans
measles traveling like a tour bus
spittle flying, coming to your town.

Bitcoin and banks going under
my money vanished
like a puff of sulfurous pollution
except for the bills hidden
between my mattress and box spring
guarded by my magic wand.

Mobs going door-to-door
marking your home with pink triangles
a slippery omen of death
why mess with what worked before.

Newspapers, white-washed
stories and the truth floating out to sea
in clumsy paper boats…sinking
their pirate flags tattered.

Spying on my minuscule words
through texts, messages, and posts
are landlines the new escape hatch

should I seal my lips with fear?

The air, the air that I breathe
it's a dirge from earth
we're broken…icebergs dissolving
I eat clouds and rain
I eat ghosts and demons
wanting to find love in the molten dirt.

I'm fearful, but am comforted by pleasure
bossa nova and squash galettes
worn corduroy pants and languorous cats
my ink-stained fingers and long-arm staplers
vaccine runs to the pharmacy before January.

I'm not afraid of naming the excess
that's clogging this country's gullet
thanksgiving in a garbage disposal
spilling out, potatoes and turkey rising
covering the kitchen floor, sticky gelatinous.

I want to be fearless
a pirate
less haunted by the future
our paths wind through the underbrush
we meet by the pond
campfire simmering and hot
seeking shelter, finding ourselves
beneath the brambles.

A Dream Year Instead of Politics

In my dreams
I'm spending this year
lolling on a tufted purple velvet chaise
indolent and sultry
time has stopped
it's endless teatime
cream puffs, tea cakes, and pirogi
my lover and I feed one another
crumbs, by kiss, by caress
a shadowed abyss of pleasure
our cats join us when we sleep
the sun setting in lurid pinks and golds
as we bathe in silvery moonlight.

Fuck this
you can't touch us
we live in splendor
our cunts beat like bird wings
flying
blood swelling and flesh hot
we're ready for you now
war drums summoning
calling, calling us to watch you
fuck this, you can't touch us.

Paradise is Burning

It's San Francisco on a Thursday
wildfire season
Paradise is burning
Union Square; 6pm
scooters, hoverboards rush by
swerving around us
silent disregard.

Stepping around flattened
cardboard sidewalk beds
bankruptcy sale signs
drunks slurring their anger.

Hotel workers drumming and striking
voices rocketing through downtown
a national demonstration
against politics
down the street
at City Hall
with its gilded dome.

I can smell Paradise burning
as I leave Trader Joe's
riding the streetcar home
past pockets of people carrying signs
stomping as we drive by
the thick smell of burnt wildlife and forests
winding through the streetcar

ghosts of bunnies and birds
fight for room
I'm nearly home
another day awash with smoke and rage.

The Violet Swan Samovar

After he won the election
I bought a Persian samovar
towering, electrical, elegant
with gilded garish flowers
and a violet swan on the front
black plastic handles
so *gashang* that my heart pounded
with love and anxiety.

I invited my friends over
to play revolutionary
we drank black tea, scalding our tongues
pounded our chests
recited dark desolate poetry
Loretta played the accordion
as we danced in a room-sized circle
I fell to the floor demanding to be
passed around, arms-to-arms
held like Jane Bowles or a cat
loved, safe.

We ate small rich cakes
flavored with cardamom
dabbing the crumbs with worn hankies
coding our desires
in a feral way
so that we couldn't forget.

We wrote a million manifestos
ending in tears
another million ending in rage
farewells because we're revolutionaries
the rain splattering the streets with dreams
goodbye for the night
then home jiggety jig.

I love you in the beautiful darkness.
our hands clasped together
fingers intertwined like seaweed
winding sidewalks lit with jasmine
panties strewn from one end of the city
to the other
flagging our flesh, open and wet
revolutionaries swimming through the stars.

Beer-Soused

Will the beer-soused squalling
of tech-bros across the street
become an enamored memory
dredging up the scent
of Hayes Valley in 2016
with unfinished projects and my cat
a pot of curry
the smell snaking through my apartment
me in my overalls
wondering about the future.

George Jones "He Stopped Loving Her Today" is
playing
I'm transported
it's 1979 for three minutes and seventeen seconds
Arlus fetching me grape soda at midnight
scampering across the avenue
scuffed black boots and torn jeans
her frizzy hair flying
in the cold Chicago wind.

I write about a now that is not now
a future undecided
a past temporal
a tomorrow that I invent
a you lying elegantly
across decades waiting for permanence.

Upon Walking Home at Night Past the DNA Lounge

Fiats and Coopers breed like horseflies
elegantly aggressive
shoving their way
banging against our skin
buzzing, "we are here, we are here!"
ruthlessly reminding us
of their brutality.

The night air cool and luscious
with promises of three-day weekends
perhaps a doughnut
from the All Star Cafe
to walk me the rest of the way home.

And yet I'm battered
the wee cars, the wee folk
you with your straight hair
your straight teeth and earnest bearing
swaying tight-assed stuffed with money.

I glanced at through the picture window
of a Frenchified bar
read the menu taped to the window to be sure
you are as hollow as I thought. You are.

The ghosts of drag kings
wave at me from across the street
I louche homewards
clenching a greasy envelope
sugar sprinkled across my lips
a benediction.

Remembering Want

There was a minute in the past
hidden under vines and snakes
another world of moss and earth.

Clashing
the smell of the last decade shakes me
electrical wires falling in storms
peach ice cream, ivory dish soap, dust
molting - wraps me in wings
butterflies swooping
layers of scales - ethereal.

I'm wanted
my flesh unfurling under your fingers.
we're striped raw
extinct creatures bumbling our way from Sodom
our lair laid bare by my bachelor ways.

Remembering
I was wanted once
that smell recoiling around my chest
squeezing my breath out
into the clean night air.

Transformation

I've spent a half a century
no, more
underwater
gliding through
fronds of seaweed
their slivery leaves
wrapping around my breasts
my waist, my hips.

Hiding in discarded
crab shells
brittle homes
protecting me
the dark ocean floor
filling my eyes
a comfort.

I wonder, no I marvel
about creatures
that are able to swim upwards
ocean to land
shaking off salt water
as they break the surface
spray flying
ribbons of seaweed
streaming from their limbs
breasts floating high

with the momentum
sea spray forming
clouds, white translucent
as they rise to breach
the surface.

Their eyes still filled
with oceans and darkness
barnacles loosened
water drying on their skin
in the sun
leaving maps
drawn in salt
an island where there
was a heart
a river between their legs
flowing from ocean to sky
their mouth stuffed
with clouds
rising, not rebirth
but transformation.

Lucky

I want to be the lucky one
a horseshoe away from a four leaf clover
a spill of salt tossed underhanded
over your shoulder and sprinkling
like snow over the top of Mt. Damavand.

I want to be that's-mister-lucky-to-you
the one who wakes up to baking bread
sweet melting sugar and butter
cotton sheets clinging to me
and you bring me buns in the morning.

I want to be Mister Luck-be-a-lady-tonight
that horse will never win, but she does
rounding the bend, a fairy leprechaun
lucky like Mercury, so speedy
around the world in 80 heartbeats.

I want to be lucky
the left hand of sinister
always reaching higher to the darkness
my lucky brain, my lucky feet, my lucky cunt,
my lucky eyes, my lucky soul, my lucky heart.

Princes and Kings

For B., who wanted to be a boy from the start

I imagine you
ten years old and laying in your bed
on a single mattress with white cotton sheets
the breeze blows the window's curtain open
letting in the cool night air, smelling of ozone.

You take one small fingertip
your skin bathed, new and soft
smelling of Ivory soap and clean fingernails
touch your jaw, pressing in to discover the
structure of your body
your face, the muscles, the epidermis, the blood,
the pores
you touch, wishing to find hair, sprouts whirling
to the surface
the smallest beard resting on your chin like a
crown.

You are a prince
you have traveled distances
and now you rest between, always between
36 years later, you stroke your chin
eking out the differences between child and adult.

I'll hunt a pelt for you
take your dream and cover you with it tenderly
smoothing, caressing your warm flesh
wanting so much.

You'll find it between day and night
between fragments of time
jumbled until linearity is unimportant
the ozone of thunderclap and change
lifting you, a growling bear
face raised and hair bristling
your beard growing, growing.

You laying in your bed
me, touching your jaw with my bathed fingertip
the graying crown
we are the kings we dreamed of.

Home

I've become a shadow of an idea
a half-baked notion sliding into the street
like debris
loose, dusty
a tangle of wires
which is my new favorite word
next to "fuck you!"

Porsches, Mini Coopers, and Fiats
rich people in the cars park
next to homeless people
sleeping on the sidewalk
homeless or not
see if home-is-where-the-heart-is
at the very least
home is where your change of underwear and bar
of soap live
home is the sidewalk.

We might ask, "Where do you live?"
five feet from the intersection of Oak and
Octavia,
next to the broken tree
between your dog's shit that you didn't pick
up
and the discarded IKEA chair.

Where is your beautiful life?
I'm looking out of
my second floor apartment window
the swaying trees
seaweed leaves in the breeze
fog tangled in the fronds
the full moon rising, my streetlight
I see you sleeping tattered
hungry beneath my window
on your cement sidewalk home
as techies pounce from Avalon next door
stepping delicately over you
watching their phones
solemn faces reflected
me in my castle above the sidewalk
my tears salting your bed.

Salt

There's an over in the attic
an ending of special places – covered.

Covered like a pie on a summer day
cobwebs sticky lace
over things that are under.

I can't name what's hidden;
is it nameless, or am I mute?
The first name of sadness is you and
the surname of sadness is salt.

I cry, my face soaked with salt
spilling over
until I'm floating like a bathing beauty
Johnny Weissmuller naked
or with a tattered loincloth

waving with a wrinkled palm – upwards
the queen of the jungle
waving hello and good-bye.

Grief has a direction and
it is inwards
washing my heart
an astringent scrubbing
the gritty purification of tears.

The Opposite of Bitter is Not You

The opposite of bitter is not you
a sweet taste in my mouth
I spit it out
musty and flavored
like something kept in the attic.

You approach me in emails
you approach me in texts
you approach me on webcam
each time, I flee.

Each message starts like you never met me
we are sitting across one another
in a dive in another country
a place where I can
only understand every thirtieth word.

I cup your chin in my palm
to look at you
but all I can see is your ass
we both look down
forgetting every thirtieth conversation
every thirtieth rendezvous.

I spit you out
I can't have this mouthful
of ass and forgotten words
rolling around my tongue like a gumball

candy I never had in my childhood.

Spit you into the wind
into another world where monsters live
all teeth and matted hair
mouth-to-mouth, spitting broken teeth
blood pooling under my tongue
coating each slippery sentence.

You are my bitter bear
an animal living in the hole
under my heart
I swallow
my drool drips warm and succulent
you lay in a pool of me
sprawled askew and tender
so sweet.

Clinging

We have clung
together this past year
not Walt Whitman
but you and I
and the world, in battle
c-words this morning
crushed, covid, coup, comorbidities.

Our apartment a cave
crowded, dark, and warm
sweetly sheltering us
I send pictures of my cat
into the world
for courage - and she is love
soaring as only an elderly cat
ruff and tail fluffed
white whiskers erect - can soar.

And we two, cooking, crying, and waiting
for safety and surrender
the battle over, we imagine
birds singing, we'll stroll
slowly, so slowly
drinking coffee inside cafes
masks off and swallowing
shocked into wonderment
our eyes blinking - are we really here?

like infant woodland creatures
we're downy-haired, unsteady and wary
hand-in-hand
breathing in the green spring air.

Masked on the 35th Day

Muffled conversation at 5pm
you in the fox mask and me wearing lovebirds
the sidewalk in front of the post office deserted
except for one lone middle aged man
balding, angry, and hurried
his mask worn behind his head
useless.

You stand close to me
far less than the recommended six feet
and murmur that you need my fingers
inside you to come
the syllables linger
humid inside your mask
pleasure released into the air
a wispy puff of dandelion.

Two crows sit overhead, squawking
making their plans for dinner
clouds scurry towards dusk
the sky threads of salmon, white, and blue
hand-in-hand we check our post office box
day 35 of the quarantine.

The Joy of Hunger
For Andy, with affection

Andy and I sat on the concrete stoop
the South end of Columbus
in the summertime
gravel crumbling on the step's edges
our cigarette butts
tossed by the metal porch rail
our knees touching, leaning into each other
her plump tanned golden leg
next to my thin fish-belly white leg
her pregnancy swollen ankle
next to my bony bug-bitten ankle
hungry, but flat broke
our boyfriends shooting up the grocery money
inside the house.

The *Joy of Cooking* open
one page on her lap and one on mine
reading out loud
our eyes watering with hunger
our stomachs cramped,
smoking to forget.

I've never cared much for green beans
preferring limas
sweet peas or eggplant
but right then I wanted green beans with bacon
fresh green beans

the kind that smelled of damp earth
not tins from the mark-down bin
bacon all salty — in meaty chunks
abundant on my tongue
between my teeth.

We sat turning each page
lingering, smoking
each exhale a sigh
wanting carrot cake and quiche
roast chicken, hot with juices
as we carved it open
our fingers skimming the paper
as we read each ingredient out loud
our stomachs hollow
legs pressed into one another
hunger spilling onto the pages
smoking cigarettes and eating dreams.

Driftwood

Unwrapped, the paper crinkled
as you picked at the tape
sticky, careful not to tear
with your soft fingers
the marbleized end paper
in seaweed greens
facile and delicate.

Inside, a staff of driftwood
dry, bumpy with knots
aged by sea and sand
peeling thin sheets of bark
they float beneath our feet
showing a nougat
of moss in the center
alive and verdant.

We reveal our spongy
hearts. Not onion layers
but lush candy
first the beauty
then the hardness
tempered by age
finally plush velvet
loamy and fresh
cradled in your palm.

The Matador and the Mouse

The matador was flashy
twirling satin
in house colors, bold
her red cape a wing
sprouting effortlessly
from her hand
to entice the bull.

The field mouse
sable brown coat
long tail swishing
traveled from her
country home
to the colosseum
living on hot dog crumbs
driblets of stale beer
silently watching.

After months of observation
the field mouse
decided to play
with the bull
so she ran to the arena floor
flap-flap, paws rising
clouds of dust
pink nose twitching
in excitement.

She hopped onto the bull
scurrying up his leg
that powerful muscle
rippling with
sweat and blood
from the matador's gores
at that moment
the bull distracted
by the red cape
a swishing wing
of fire - glorious.

The mouse climbed up
claws clinging
to the bull's head
to nestle in his ear
incisors sharpened
biting softly at first
a quiet battle
then finally burrowing
into the bull's ear
through his brain
only to pop up
in the bull's eye
coated in the bulls death
triumphant and wet
a bullseye, as the bull
toppled onto the arena sand
dead.

Bilious Dreams

And me with a cold on the sofa
unable to really wake up
with any resemblance of lucidity
the rain pouring as if it were snow
us in the winter of 2016.

I want to keep it simple
so my snot fogged brain can focus
treason, coups, Russia, and you
bile roils in my belly
a pain that I walk off
eating hanks of white bread
to soak up the acid.

We're here in December
incomplete and grieving
petitions, calls, postcards, marches
knowing we are moving forward
forward to a bleak still lake of tears
I bake cake, hug my cat
dreams struggle to the surface
it's difficult
not to fall in line
with a random conspiracy theory.

Maybe the truth is simply what I see;
you leaving this world
your fate cast with ballots

fluttering like ravens over your heart
carrion, seeking a bitter morsel
devoid of blood, from some deal
you made when you thought you would win
everything, and you never did
62 million give or take a spy or two
you toss the cards aside to leave the game
unaware that you're past the point
of quitting, gliding into the future
red necktie rippling from the breeze
of river water rising to the surface
no words left
bereft of comprehension.

Tempered

I'm becoming tempered
a piece of stolen glass
a splinter in a shoe
life and death working their bloody entrance
into my body.

I remember the smell of molten metals
the hiss of acids at the jewelers
poured over silver and gold
heat
the smell clogging my throat
until I couldn't breathe
tempered.

And you – you die
a sudden crash
the fire extinguished
the splinter inside traveling towards the heart
the beating hand like a bird wing
a song - something that is missing.

Another with an overdose
you with a broken aorta
you die in bed
you step on a landmine
you slam into a tree
you removed from life support
each a sliver.

The glass inside my heart
splintering into millions of pieces
traveling throughout my body
inside my flesh
broken glass, a lacy patchwork.

And yet today
I'm becoming tempered
life and death
your cane by the door
days-of-the-week medicine
but really —
you fucking me slowly
me coming, flowing upwards
roaring into a sailor pillow
you whisper, "dude, sweet"
we sleep together
once again, I'm tempered.

Thoughts I Never Knew I Had

Sometimes my thoughts are oblique
they slither out of my mouth like river snakes
long green bodies tickling my lips
they're harmless, I suppose
but with a sneaky grace.

There are some snakes that hibernate
they stay in my cranium
curled up and seemingly sleeping
waiting to dance in my dreams
or to live in words written in invisible ink
letters written in a mirror.

Your words rise and fall,
your voice through the wires
your face and chest, an image on my monitor
your words rise and fall
like grape soda through a straw
the purple bubbles foaming towards my mouth
my lips sucking you in
you say "hot" and now I'm wet.

I know what I want
my snakes are here in my open palm
you say "hot", and now I'm wet
I'm holding them out to you – a gift
they wave coolly to you
you are a snake-charmer in a fairy tale

or they are ocean foliage
it all comes back to water
you smile, open mouthed and tongue tip showing
your hands reaching out.

I swear there are no hidden snakes in my skull
plaited together, waiting to unravel their stories
dozing in the heat of my head – slumbering
and I believe myself
knowing that the unexpected is just a drop of
blood away
that this is how stories are written
in invisible ink and in a mirror
I believe myself
you say "hot" and now I'm wet.

Desire

I only wanted a single thing
traveling through my body
indistinct and soft;
the leaves of the weeping cherry tree
through twelve panes of glass
turning to October
birds crackling across the street
my feet tingling with age
you sleeping next to me
a baby bear with silver hair
snoring as lightly as a soufflé
your paws grope blindly
our skin meets in the morning.

I only wanted a single thing

Pandemic Lockdown on a Tuesday Morning

There is one lone bumblebee
lurching from flower to flower
drunkenly in the May rain
8am — no rush hour traffic
no cars pulling from the driveway
no car doors slamming and broken mufflers
birdsong muffled by raindrops.

I'm reminded of the soft thump
of rolled up newspapers hitting stoops
and find myself listening for the news
but that was a half a century ago
now I browse each morning on my phone
scents of ink, coffee, and rain
a memory falling from the sky.

Slow Hand Coup, 2021

Although it was a coup
everything started slowly
months before
not quick and hard the way you'd think
hot coffee, warm cat, and a girlfriend in bed
no snow outside
one Georgia win announced
hoping for a second.

Later a mushroom omelet
learning to not accept substitutions
for fresh mushrooms
during curbside grocery shopping
then therapy via zoom
we processed desire during covid
laughing.

Afterwards, work in my home office
the cat sleeping beside me
the news at the ready
a repetitive pandemic life
Wednesday waiting to burst open
into an attempted coup.

Time greedily eats its own tail
the past is the future, is the now
regurgitating every death and leave taking
until we're left only with videos of traitors

fists raised
hands touching one another across the centuries
clouds of smoke billow.

Whose smoke — our smoke
whose house — our house
whose death — our death.

Sunday in the Park

It's a San Francisco spring
mid Sunday morning
the park paths
are flooded with dykes.

In Golden Gate Park
we meander lazily
scatter crumbs for ducks
nap in a bower
the sun golden and lush.

Hummus and carrot cake
faded quilts over clover
shoes off, bellies bare
the smell of hot skin.

Bees collect nectar
while squirrels frolic
couples smooch
the light blessing them
with a swoon of sweetness.

The scent of blossoms
flesh rolling, undulating
salty sweat - desire
talking and walking.

A guitarist softly
plays songs of courage and love
her voice tender and strong
we hold her - rub her feet
sing the chorus.

Remember this day
this is resistance
blankets of warm grass
a picnic, a poem, a kiss.

Trannyboi Sailor

For Carol Queen and her trannyboi sailor

There is a picture of a trannyboi sailor
in my bedroom
strong chin and wide lips
round blue-eyed with dark lashes
peeking at me shyly.

A sailor cap on his head
navy middy over his chest
beneath it is his heart
an organ wrapped in music
his beating heart sings "You Go To My Head"
I get teary-eyed listening
to his sighs and pleas.

He whispers in my ear
"you intoxicate me with your eyes"
it is enough to make me spread my legs
let the seafaring world in
there are angels and baby birds.
mermaids and seaweed
sway to his whispers.

My robe is covered in spades
I have a halo of wings
lean forward to touch his face
my fingers as translucent as clouds
my palm resting, open on his flushed cheek

lips parted softly for a kiss
a seafaring journey.

500 Words

You carry five hundred words for liar
your backpack bursting
open, gaping
the metal zippers failing
its teeth snapping
crocodile – sharp as knives.

Here, you hold my head
my mouth open
as you force your lies
down my throat
your rough hands
hairy and relentless
stinking of cigars and greed.

There're so many lies
that they back up
dripping from my nostrils
my eyes watering
I struggle to breathe
the words choke me
syllables and verbs
you throttle the world.

I want to hear
with my little ear
I mock my softness

disallow my need
I want to hear
five hundred and one
words for truth-teller.

You're uninterested
I beg for truth
you're uninterested in truth
you grab another fistful of lies
oozing between your meaty fingers
rotten, putrid
finished.

The Lion and the Lamb

What is beside the other?
the stitches purled
when knitting.

The lion and the lamb
when frolicking.

The cat and the mouse
when chasing.

The moon and the sun
when orbiting.

Together, tied tenderly together.
And me, what am I tied to?
when frolicking
when chasing
when orbiting.

A hank of forgetfulness
a clench of pearls
good manners and bravery out the window
I yearn for to be tied
together, tied tenderly together.

Sequestered, 2021

Some variety of icy rain and slush
a mug of cooling coffee
a grocery list that exists in my head
for candlelit dinners
I write recipes in my pandemic journal
blessing my forethought in buying a fancy pen.

My wishes savory and sweet,
sour and sticky
meet upon my tongue
it's just us two in my dreamtime;
we laugh across the table
serving salads and *khoresh*
reaching for more
our hands brushing one another
electric, skin to skin
although the world is ending.

Today I'm sequestered in my apartment
searching for curbside pickup and deliveries
to avoid stores, disease and death
because GOP = genocide
and I'd like to have a choice in how I die
not tipped over
like a shrub with loosened roots
flung upwards
you fucker.

Another sip of coffee
I write;
fondue, baked brie, spice cake
lull me into deep breathing
just a few more months
we can do this.

I've discovered that
the local farm delivery service
does not deliver butch farmers
to your doorstep
with overalls, tattooed biceps, mused hair
tender eyes - looking for kisses and cake
but delivers beets, sriracha, eggs, and mushrooms
I'm deeply disappointed
but not surprised
not surprised at all.

New Year's Potluck

The New Year came and went
at a potluck at June's home
laced with clouds of pot
cigars, wine
left-over holiday food
in orange pottery bowls.

There were women - warm
partially undressed in the kitchen
removing casseroles from the oven
their discarded clothing draped on chairs
laughing over their shoulder at me
hair disheveled
cheeks pink from the heat.

I leaned against the wall covered
with portraits of the city
naked women, breast asunder
stuck up willy-nilly with red thumb-tacks
the artist had drawn most of them
traded for the rest
women talked loudly and sweetly
each hot-pad covered hand held promise
kneeling women's backs shone
as their pants rode down
shirts gathered up
kneeling, bare backs all warm and fleshy
sometimes with a pantie rim

a sliver of moon showing the way
all shining and bright
look here, this is where you need to go next.

I leaned against the kitchen wall
waited for the year to begin
waited to find you with flushed cheeks
laughter coming towards me
breast asunder and hands reaching.

At Night

We loved many things
but never rainbows and unicorns
never glitter and cupcakes
we're bristly bears
guarding our hearts.

Stepping out at night.
the moon a smog covered beam
of something straight to the heart
you take my hand as we cross the street
nervously bumping hips until
padded we touch delicate
hand-in-hand
and forget to move away.

Sleek

A glooming, stream of dreams
I fall for you
I fall tripping
over fruit sloppy strewn
along my path, and over
and over I fall.

The night air a fog
a mist amorphous
winding its way
through me
like I wasn't there, wasn't there.

Your fingers are pointed branches
thorned and barren
a whisper touching scraping
my arm as I slide
falling for you, and you
are the clouds, the wind
the sleet driving the hail
like small knives into my chest
sideways, I sleek into the dirt.

Maps

It's early springtime
snowdrops and birdsong
surround us as we
watch for emigrants
at Paradise Pond
near where the pathway ends.

A smoke spiral overhead
guides us. To
their campfire
where five people
three children, wary
sit beside a dented tin percolator
perched over their fire
brewing coffee, sweat, grime
all mingling with the
morning dew.

We open our knapsacks
to share breakfast
bread and cheese
apples from last fall
and gather
unfold our maps
guiding paths
that follow the Mill River
to safe houses.

This pathway
has been walked
by ghosts
decades ago, no centuries
protecting their flight
rivers and railroads
mapping their way to home.

Now red to blue
running, stumbling
over rocks and moss
in spring
marked by maple sap lines
their existence hidden
shoved into bags waiting
for snowdrops and birdsong
to unfurl
the wind carrying our song.

www.ingramcontent.com/pod-product-compliance
Lightning Source LLC
Chambersburg PA
CBHW030011010826
48973CB00009B/2754